First published 2018 by Walker Books Ltd
87 Vauxhall Walk, London SE11 5HJ

1 2 3 4 5 6 7 8 9 10

Text © 2018 Vivian French Illustrations © 2018 Salvatore Rubbino

This book has been typeset in M Klang

Printed in China

British Library Cataloguing in Publication Data: a catalogue
record for this book is available from the British Library

ISBN 978-1-4063-7291-5

www.walker.co.uk

For Ivy, with much love
Gran xxx

To Yvette, David and Huw
S.R.

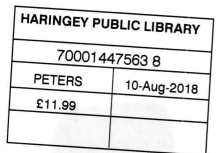

WE'RE GETTING A
CAT!

VIVIAN FRENCH

illustrated by

SALVATORE RUBBINO

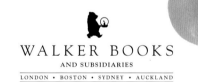

WALKER BOOKS
AND SUBSIDIARIES
LONDON • BOSTON • SYDNEY • AUCKLAND

OUR family got a cat because my dad is terrified – and
I mean TERRIFIED! – of mice.

We didn't have them when we lived in the centre of town.
But then we moved to a new flat in an old house ... and it had
LOADS of mice.

We'd only been there two weeks when he stomped into the
kitchen and said, "We're getting a cat!"

Mum said, "But you don't like cats!"

"Cats catch mice," said Dad. "I like them now.
I like them very much."

So that weekend
we went to the home
for rescue cats –
and we chose Kevin.

"He's big and strong," Dad said. "He'll catch all the mice."

A week later Kevin was allowed
to come home with us,
and me and my sister
were SO HAPPY!

Someone will come from the rescue centre to make
sure you and your cat are right for each other,
and to answer any questions you might have.

Mrs Harris next door had a cat, so we asked her how to make
Kevin feel at home.

"Keep him inside for at least three weeks," she said. "If you let
him go outside too soon he'll try to run back to where he came from.
He needs to get used to the idea that he's your cat." She paused.
"Oh, and he'll need a litter tray. I've got an old one you can use."

A litter tray isn't a wastepaper basket — it's a cat's indoor toilet!

We went to the pet shop and bought some special grainy stuff
to put in the tray. Then we put the tray in the cupboard
in the hall and propped the door open.
Kevin went straight in, and did a wee.

Cat poo can carry nasty germs, so always wear gloves
when you clean out the litter tray. It's best to clean
it out every day. Always wash your hands as well!

11

Me and my sister made Kevin a lovely bed in a cardboard box,
but he didn't like it much. He slept on top of the fridge, the back
of the sofa and the pile of newspapers waiting to be recycled.

In the evenings he came and kept us company, and if Dad was there he always wanted to sit on his knee. At first Dad shooed him away, but after a few days he said, "Pesky cat. But at least he knows who's important."

Mum rolled her eyes.

Cats have minds of their own. They can't be trained like dogs. They like to make their own decisions!

It was fun finding out about cats. But sometimes we got things wrong...

Kevin hated having his tummy tickled. When we tried he went to sit with his back to us, his tail twitching. Mrs Harris said it meant he was cross.

He didn't like having his fur brushed the wrong way.

Some cats love being stroked and cuddled, and some cats hate it. RESPECT your cat's feelings! It'll love you all the more.

He didn't like being wheeled about in my sister's dollies' pram.

He didn't like the water in his bowl. He liked the water in the toilet better. We were worried it was dirty, but Mrs Harris said it was all right – and Kevin drank it.

Try catching rainwater in a bucket for your cat to drink. They should always have water available ... but NOT cow's milk. It's not good for them!

What did Kevin like?

He liked curling up beside me and head-butting me until I scratched his ears.

He liked cleaning himself all over (especially in between his toes).

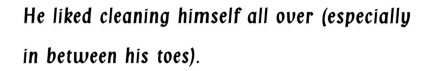

He liked chasing a pingpong ball, or a piece of paper on the end of a string.

He liked sitting at the window
and making growly noises
at the pigeons.

He liked scratching
the back of Mum's chair.
We didn't tell Mum.
We used our pocket money
to buy him a scratching
post. Dad helped us a bit!

Cats scratch anything they think is suitable to keep their
claws sharp. A scratching post will save the furniture!

17

Most of all, Kevin liked eating.

He ate all the food we put in his bowl, and he purred a lot.

Cats are carnivores (meat-eaters) and they need meat to stay healthy. Use good quality tinned cat food, and follow the instructions on the tin or ask your vet for advice.

After a week, he knew he was fed at eight in the morning and six in the evening, and he would rush into the kitchen and sit by his bowl.

Put your cat's food and water in separate shallow bowls. They like to be able to see round them while they eat ... and they don't like their whiskers brushing the sides!

We loved Kevin. The only
problem was he didn't catch
any mice. And that made
Dad VERY grumpy.

One night the mice were extra
noisy and kept Dad awake for AGES.
He was scowling as he ate his breakfast.
"That cat's useless," he said. "He's
got to go!"

And he stomped off to work.

When we told Mrs Harris about it, she shook her head. "Poor Kevin. Maybe he doesn't like catching mice."

"Isn't that what cats do?" I asked.

"Some cats aren't bothered," Mrs Harris said. "Especially if they're used to having regular meals."

"But Dad's going to send him away," my sister wailed.

"No he's not." Mum sounded very firm. "Kevin's part of our family now. He's staying."

"But what about the mice?" I asked.

"You could try mint," Mrs Harris said. "Or there are other ways to get rid of them..."

Kevin was stretching out his paws to admire his claws. And Mrs Harris smiled.

"Is he cleaning himself a lot? That means he's settling in nicely. Well done!"

Cats groom themselves to keep their fur in good condition. Healthy fur keeps them warm in winter, and extra grooming keeps them cool in summer.

My sister beamed. "Do you think he can go out now? It's three weeks today since we got him."

"Let him out this evening, just before his teatime," Mrs Harris suggested. "And rattle his kitty crunchie box when you call him back in."

Nearly all cats are happiest if they can go outdoors. A cat flap means they can go in and out when they want.

We let Kevin out at half past five. He strolled out of the door as if he wasn't bothered whether he was in or out, but then he leapt over the garden wall and vanished.

My sister burst into tears. "He's run away!"

"We'll give him five minutes, and then we'll rattle his kitty crunchie box," Mum said. "He'll come rushing back for his tea."

But he didn't. We rattled and called for ages, but there was no sign of Kevin. Even Mum looked worried.

Dad got home at half past six. "Hello!" he said. "You all look miserable! What's up?"

"Kevin's run away!" my sister wailed.
"He knew you didn't want him, and he's gone!"

"No he hasn't," Dad said. "He was sitting on the front path waiting for me. Look!"

And in walked Kevin, purring loudly.

27

IF YOU'RE GETTING A CAT

Cats can live until they're twenty (that's about 96 in human years) or even older, so if you're thinking about getting a cat, make sure you're ready to have a furry friend for a long, long time!

To keep your cat happy and healthy, he or she will need to be vaccinated against cat diseases – and it's important to keep the vaccinations up to date. They'll need regular worming (at least four times a year) and do watch out for fleas – your local pet shop will have treatments to get rid of them, or you can ask your vet. Cats can get lost, too, so a microchip (they don't hurt!) will make sure they can be easily identified and come home to you. Collars can catch on tree branches so make sure to buy one with an elastic bit so the cat can escape.

Choose your cat carefully; you're adopting a new (and very special) member of the family ... and remember: cats are WONDERFUL!

INDEX

Look up the pages to find out about all these cat things. Don't forget to look at both kinds of word – **this kind** and *this Kind*.

USEFUL WEBSITES

www.pdsa.org.uk or **www.bluecross. org.uk** have all the information you're likely to need.

If you've got a problem with mice, **goodhousekeeping.com** has lots of advice.